Sleepy
Polar Bear

written by
Monica Hiris

illustrated by
Jerry Harston

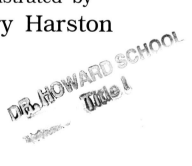

It was a hot sunny day.
Children were coming to
spend the day at the zoo.

2

3

The monkeys were climbing.

The seals were swimming.

The tigers were playing,

but the polar bear...

...just slept.

The monkeys were chattering.

The lions were roaring.

The parrots were talking,

...just slept.

The monkeys were swinging.

The penguins were diving.

The giraffes were eating,

but the polar bear...

...just slept.

ZZZZZZZ

As the children watched, the polar bear yawned, stretched out his paws, lifted his head, and opened his eyes.

Then the great big polar bear...

...rolled over!